TOO MUCH TROUBLE
FOR
GRANDPA

Rob Lewis

First published in the United States of America in 1998
by **MONDO Publishing**
Originally published in the United Kingdom in 1997
by The Bodley Head Children's Books,
an imprint of Random House UK Ltd.

For information contact:
MONDO Publishing
One Plaza Road
Greenvale, New York 11548

Visit our web site at http://www.mondopub.com

Printed in Hong Kong
First Mondo Printing, August 1997
97 98 99 00 01 02 03   9 8 7 6 5 4 3 2 1

Library of Congress Cataloging-in-Publication Data
Lewis, Rob, 1962-
    Too much trouble for Grandpa / Rob Lewis.
        p.   cm.
    "Originally published in the United Kingdom in 1997 by the Bodley Head
Children's Books, an imprint of Random House UK Ltd."—Copyr. p.
    Summary: Finley's Grandpa acquires a series of companions, including a
finicky cat named Elvis, a new girlfriend, and a clever talking bird, but each one
presents problems for Grandpa and Finley.
    ISBN 1-57255-551-3 (pbk : alk. paper)
    [1. Bears—Fiction. 2. Grandfathers—Fiction. 3. Pets—Fiction.] I. Title.
PZ7.L58785To   1998
[E]—dc21   97-14197
                                                              CIP
                                                              AC

ELVIS

Finley sat in Grandpa's best chair.

They were watching the sports show

on television.

It was their favorite program.

"What would you like for supper?"

asked Grandpa.

"Hot dogs please," said Finley.

"You always want hot dogs," said

Grandpa.

"They're my favorite," said Finley.

After supper Grandpa and Finley went

for a drive.

Grandpa's car was very old.
It didn't even have a roof.
Finley liked it very much.

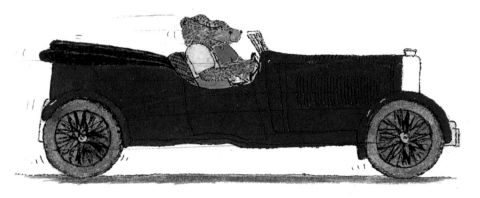

A cat crossed the road in front of
the car.

"I'm getting a cat," said Grandpa.
"You are too busy for pets," said Finley.
"Cats are no trouble," said Grandpa.

The next week, Finley went to Grandpa's house.

"This is Elvis," said Grandpa.

"Hello," said Finley.

"HSSSSS!" said Elvis.

"He is very friendly," said Grandpa.

"He doesn't *look* friendly," said Finley.

Elvis went into the living room.

He sat on the best chair.

"That's *my* chair," said Finley crossly.

"HSSSSS!"

said Elvis.

"Elvis likes that chair," said Grandpa.

Finley sat on the floor. It was time for

their favorite television program.

"HSSSSS!"

said Elvis.

"Elvis doesn't like sports," said Grandpa. "Let's have supper instead."

Elvis sat at the table with Grandpa and Finley.

"Can we have hot dogs again?" asked Finley.

"No," said Grandpa. "Elvis doesn't like hot dogs. We are having fish."

"Oh," said Finley. He didn't like fish very much.

After supper Grandpa and Finley
washed the dishes.

"Can we go for a drive now?"
asked Finley.

"Not this evening," said Grandpa.
"Elvis needs his worming pills."

"That won't take long," said Finley.

"It will," said Grandpa. "Elvis doesn't
like worming pills."

Finley went home.

Visiting Grandpa wasn't much fun with
Elvis there.

But the next week Elvis was gone.

"Cats are too much trouble," said
Grandpa.

"Good!" said Finley.

"And Mavis doesn't like cats," Grandpa
added.

"Who is Mavis?" asked Finley.

"My new girlfriend," said Grandpa proudly.

Finley's eyes opened very wide.

"Grandpas don't have girlfriends," he said.

Grandpa grinned. "Girlfriends are no trouble," he said.

"Hello!" said Mavis.

"Hello," said Finley.

They went into the living room.

Mavis sat in the best chair.

Finley turned
on the television.

"Oh good!" said Mavis. "*Crimebusters* is on."

"I was going to watch the sports show," said Finley.

"Mavis doesn't like sports," said Grandpa.

15

After *Crimebusters* they had supper.

"Are we having hot dogs?" Finley asked hopefully.

Mavis made a face.

"Mavis doesn't eat meat," said Grandpa. "She is a vegetarian."

"Does she eat fish?" asked Finley.

"No," said Grandpa. "Only vegetables."

"That's a relief," said Finley.

"We are having parsnip stew," said
Grandpa. Finley didn't like parsnip
stew very much either.

After supper Grandpa and Finley
washed the dishes.

"Can we go for a drive?" asked Finley.

"Mavis doesn't like drives," said Grandpa sadly. "They make her carsick."

"Mavis is less fun than Elvis," grumbled Finley. "I bet she takes worming pills, too!"

"Don't be silly," said Grandpa.

"Pass me my pills, dear!"

called Mavis.
Grandpa gave Finley a funny look.

SHELF TROUBLE

Grandpa and Finley were visiting
Mavis.

Mavis stomped about in the kitchen.
Then she clattered the dishes.

"Uh oh!" said Finley. "Mavis is in a
bad mood."

"It must be the weather," said Grandpa.

Mavis had a headache. She went
upstairs to rest.

"We will have to cheer her up,"
said Finley.

"We could do the dishes," suggested
Grandpa.

"Dishes are no fun," said Finley.

"We could hang the laundry out to dry," said Grandpa.

"It's raining outside," said Finley.

"We could vacuum the living room," said Grandpa.

"It will make too much noise," said Finley.

Grandpa and Finley thought for a long
time. They went into the kitchen to have
a drink.

Then Grandpa had an idea.
"We could put up some shelves," he said.

"Won't that make a lot of noise?"
asked Finley.

"Not if I hammer quietly," said Grandpa.

Grandpa got some tools from the shed.

He drilled holes and hammered
quietly. He had to do a lot of
drilling and hammering before
the shelves looked straight.

"What about the other
holes?" Finley asked.
"We'll use some filler,"
said Grandpa.

Grandpa found some filler powder
under the sink.

He put the powder into a bowl and
added some water.

He mixed it with an electric mixer.

The filler sprayed around the room.

"I think the speed is too fast," said

Grandpa.

Grandpa gave up with the filler.

"I will pick some flowers for Mavis," he said. "Then she won't mind the mess."

Finley was not so sure.

He filled in some holes while Grandpa picked flowers.

When Grandpa came back they heard
a noise upstairs.

"Mavis is awake," said Grandpa.

"I must go now," said Finley.

"I have homework to do."

Finley hurried down the road.

He heard a loud noise from Mavis's
house.

Aaaaaah!

A few days later, Finley met Grandpa
in the street.
He was carrying a big box.

"Where is Mavis?" asked Finley.

"Mavis is gone," said Grandpa.

"Good," said Finley. "Girlfriends are too much trouble."

"You're right," said Grandpa. "And . . . Mavis wouldn't like Conan."

Grandpa lifted the lid of the box.

"Uh oh!" said Finley.

CONAN

Finley was looking at Conan.

"Conan is a very big bird," he said.

"Yes," said Grandpa proudly. "And he does tricks."

"Really?" said Finley.

"He can ruffle his feathers," said Grandpa.

Conan ruffled his feathers.

"That's not clever," said Finley.
"He can hang upside down,"
said Grandpa.

Conan hung upside down.
"Not bad," said Finley.
"And he can add!" said Grandpa.
"You're joking," said Finley.
"Watch," said Grandpa.

"Conan, what is three plus three?"

"Aark aark aark aark aark aark,"

said Conan.

"That *is* clever," said Finley.

"I will be famous," boasted Grandpa.

"Conan will be famous, you mean,"

said Finley.

Grandpa told his neighbor Fred about Conan.

He told the cashier at the supermarket.

He even told people at the bus stop.

On Monday Fred came to see Conan.
"The newspaper will be interested,"
he said.

On Tuesday a reporter came.

He asked Grandpa a lot of questions.

He asked Conan to do a lot of adding.

"He is a very clever bird,"

said the reporter.

On Wednesday there were lots of
reporters at the door.

They wanted pictures
of Grandpa.

They wanted pictures
of Conan.

They wanted
pictures of Grandpa
and Conan together.

The reporters asked Grandpa a lot of
questions. Grandpa was very tired.

On Thursday a television crew came.
They filmed Grandpa and Conan
all day.

"This is too much!" Grandpa said.

On Friday he took Conan back to
the pet shop.

Finley visited Grandpa in the evening.

"Where is Conan?" asked Finley.

"On the television," said Grandpa.

They watched Conan on the television.

"What is six take away two?" asked the man.

"Aark aark aark aark,"

said Conan.

Everybody clapped.

"Birds are too much trouble," said Grandpa. "Now I just have a hamster."

"Can it do tricks?" asked Finley.

"No," said Grandpa.

"That's good," said Finley.

"I can talk!"

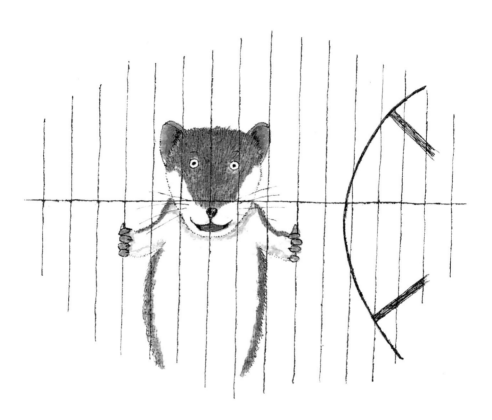

said the hamster.

"Uh oh!" said Grandpa and Finley.